SWORD
SONGS

A Collection of Fantasy Short Stories

Dean Kastle

Edits by Michael DeAngelo

Book Cover by Covers By Rio

First edition. 2024

CONTENTS

ACKNOWLEDGEMENTS

The list of friends and family who helped bring these stories to life is a long one, but I have to mention a few. Many thanks go to authors Steve Karas, Michael DeAngelo, and Lou Anders. My go-to story consultant, Dean B, gets a shout as well. Finally, my wife, life-partner, and Motivator-in-Chief, Marilyn must share the credit for every word that made it to the page.

This book is dedicated to Marilyn, who supported me, motivated me, and encouraged me to dream big.

Introduction

Dear Reader,

If you love a good fight scene, the prospect of a duel, an epic battle, gladiators, assassins, or mercenaries, then we're on the same page—literally. The purpose of the stories collected in SWORD SONGS is to have fun with this sort of tale. After each, I offer a few notes on the genesis of the story and/or how they relate to the rest of my work.

Regarding setting, all the stories contained in this collection take place in a region called Eria, the habitable lands between the frozen breath of the Hoarwinds in the north and the blasting heat of the Firons in Cauldron Sea to the south. This is the same setting as the novels in my DOG OF WAR Epic and LEGACY Cycle. With SWORD SONGS, I welcome you to this world.

In relation to my novels, all of the stories in this collection can be considered prequels, but it is not necessary to read them to understand the longer works. As such, they can be read in any order. Enjoy!

Dean Kastle

IRON AND SNOW

"Iron-Top!" a voice called. "I know you hear me, you bastard!"

Heren Iron-Top pushed up from his chair with a groan, cracked a shutter. "Uro's puckered asshole." A heavyset man with a sword stood out in front of his cottage, looking madder than a hound with the froth-mouth.

Heren didn't know how the sonofabitch had found him, but he had. He looked toward his back door, shook his head with another curse, and fetched his sword instead.

"There you are, you bastard! Time we settled an old score!"

"Which score is that?" Heren asked from his doorway. He knew he was a bad man, but he couldn't resist toying with the big lump.

"Back in the Lows, what you did to Thom and those archers..."

The fat man rambled on about some fight Heren didn't even remember. He let him say his piece. That allowed Heren time to massage his aching right shoulder. His knees didn't like the way he'd jolted up to meet this bellowing whoreson either. They didn't call him 'Iron-Top' because of his youthful vigor.

Should start calling myself Snow-Top, he was thinking. The fat man had finished his tirade, somewhat at a loss, seeing Heren's lackluster response.

He probably could have ended it right there, Heren. He could have blustered, matched the man's accusations with threats, tales of blood-curdling deeds, boasts of all the fearsome warriors he'd killed. He could have scared him off. Or maybe roughed him up a little and then let him run.

But he wasn't about to do that. He frowned instead, held the sword uncertainly at his side, moved slow, ran a hand over his white hair, tried to look anxious. He didn't do anything halfway, the old devil called Iron-Top. And he wasn't going to leave a man like this alive to come after him another day.

No, you have to finish an enemy when you have the chance.

"Look, I got no quarrel with you, brother," he said finally, stepping out into the sun. "Why don't we just let bygones be bygones, live and let live, eh?"

Of course, that only emboldened the hateful cunt, exactly the thing Heren wanted. The fat bastard came barging at him, flailing with an overhand swing. *The kind you can sidestep in your sleep.* Heren dodged but didn't counter. Instead, he pretended to move unsteadily. He didn't have to fake the pained look on his face, kneecaps protesting the sudden movement. He parried a second slash, deflected a backhand, circled once before sending back an attack of his own.

It wasn't a testing thrust—Heren was used to being faster than his enemies, stronger than they expected, better positioned, more technical—it was a thrust he knew his enemy could handle. He watched the triumph, the confidence, play across the man's face as he knocked the blow aside.

Heren deflected the counter that answered, then sent a swift cut down low at the man's thigh. The fat man reacted in time, but barely. Heren quickened his attack in increments, sent a darting thrust at the fat man's middle, then a slash at his thigh, bouncing off the parry back up toward his neck. He watched this fat bastard's expression go from confident, to angry, to unsure, to panicked.

"You sonofabitch!" The man tried to rally, tried to call on his anger.

But Heren stepped the pace up even more, cut, thrust, pivot, advance. Thrust, sidestep, advance, thrust. It was all the fat pig could do to keep his arms moving.

No breath wasted on curses now?

Heren took the man to school, careful not to strike so hard he might disarm his pupil or send him stumbling to the ground. Just hard enough to press him left, then turn him back right, then push him backwards. The hefty bastard's eyes showed white all around, the fear in them plain as day. He would have run for it then, Heren was sure. But it was all Fatty could do to dodge the thrusts and cuts of Iron-Top, the man he'd come after all on his own, because of some pathetic notion of honor or pride.

Beads of sweat ran down Heren's temple and he decided he'd had enough. He pressed until the fat man was backed all the way across the yard, up against the fence beside the road. His chickens had long since escaped, but Heren supposed the little fence was good for something.

"Ahh!"

The man wailed as a final swing knocked open his guard, exposed his middle. His eyes went even wider for that fraction of a second when he knew what was coming but could do nothing to stop it.

And it came, a ferocious backhand, slicing open his belly just below the navel. With a groan, his sword fell from his grip and both hands clutched at the glistening guts that burst like the coils of a snake through his tunic to slide down his legs.

He collapsed in a whimpering heap. Iron-Top just left him there. He turned, walked on creaky knees back inside the house.

He didn't become a feared soldier by accident, Heren Iron-Top. He'd been born a farmer, but when he left to put on Paellian white and join the army, he gave it his all. No point in doing it halfway. And it turned out he had a knack for it, rising from the rank and file all the way to captain. Should have been a marshal maybe, even a general, he'd sometimes thought, but he was just too damn good with a blade. They needed him near the action, killing people.

In the Lows, he stood in the center of the shield wall and faced the Mog charge. In Pellon itself, it was rebels they fought. And when the rebels and outlanders were quiet, the great Paellian familae fought amongst themselves. They made him Champion of the Host, a place of honor by all accounts.

There was always a score to be settled, a duel to be won. Heren fought for this man or that, killed the champions of other general's hosts, the master-at-arms of other lord's estates. Those were bloody times—the years of struggle between Familae Kion and the Leyai—until Elius and his witch queen finally secured their grip on the crown. By the time the Affliction swept over the land, killing one in three, Heren was ready for things to cool down. His knees hurt every morning and his shoulder hurt all day long. He cast off his white cloak, left the army behind. But his reputation, the deeds he'd done, they followed him. And so did his enemies.

So, he came to this far-flung town near the Lach hills. To hide, live quiet. But bastards like the fat man somehow found him even there. He wiped the man's blood from his sword and threw the rag in the fire. He found a bag, filled it with spare clothes, flint and tinder, coin, a waterskin. He set his old army bedroll beside it. It wasn't a month later another bastard came yelling out for Iron-Top. This time he picked up that bag and bedroll and left out the back.

"Where the hell am I going?" he asked the campfire, prodding it with his sword, sending a burst of embers up into the night. He almost wished he'd left the weapon. It wouldn't get him any closer to being free.

He could go back to the Lows, he mused—that's where all the other fugitives went. But if he could be found in the Lach hills, he'd be found even easier there. Probably still had enemies waiting for him, in fact.

What about Adamar? A man with a good sword arm could find employment there. But too many Paellian lords wandered in and out, for the drink and the women and the gladiatorial contests. In any case, who the hell with achy knees wanted to freeze up there by their gods-be-damned sea?

No, he reckoned he could be found just about anywhere if someone really tried. *So many old men out there, why can't they let an old snake slither under a rock? Because he's ate a few mice?*

Heren prodded the fire again and cursed. They claimed to want revenge. More than a few wanted one or another of the bounties that had been placed on him by this enemy or that. Truth be told, Heren knew most of the men that came for him were after his glory. He'd gladly have given it to them if it worked that way.

"They'll only be happy once they have my head," he muttered out loud. "I dunno why, when there's plenty of other heads out there with white hair on top."

For some reason, that started Heren laughing. It was just a snort at first, but it turned to giggles, then side-aching guffaws as an idea sprang to mind. *Could it actually work?*

The thought sobered him in an instant. Maybe it could. He wiped the tears, sat there thinking. Then he nodded. He didn't waste time but packed up and started toward the next village.

It took a few weeks, but he found what he needed by and by.

"You say he's sick?" Heren asked the barman at a little roadside inn called the Spoon and Kettle.

"Tolvan?" The barman shook his head, sighed. "Sure is. Reckon he's for the grave soon enough. Why'd you ask?"

"Because," Heren had been using the same pretense for a while now and his words were well practiced. "I'm one of Vorda's own. They might have need of a cleric, say some words, perform the rites. And dig the grave."

The barman brightened. "Well, that would be kind of you. I don't imagine his folk will have much in the way of coin to offer a holy-man—"

"No, no." Heren raised both hands. "I couldn't accept anyway. It's part of the path to wisdom. A hot meal is all I ask."

Everyone knew the Dark Lady's clerics would work for a song, but the barman smiled anyway. Heren left with directions to the dying man's home. He walked at a healthy clip despite his groaning knees, and before long stood knocking at the front door.

A gaunt-faced old woman answered. "Who are you?"

"I'm an old friend of Tolvan's," Heren lied. "From the army."

"The army?"

"He never told you he fought in the wars?"

The old woman burst into tears and Heren found she'd leaned into his shoulder, quivering. He held her best he could, patted her back. Least he could do. Even a snake warms up after some time under the sun.

"Well, you're too late," she said finally. "I'm sorry to say, but he's dead already. How did you even hear he was sick?"

"We old soldiers, word travels far and fast among our lot." *Farther than I wish.* "Came quick as I could."

The old woman wiped her eyes, pushed open the door and motioned Heren inside. "He's in there."

Heren moved through the sparsely furnished cottage, ducking around dried herbs hung from low rafters. The sight of Tolvan—whoever he was—was almost enough to make Heren cry.

Tears of joy, of course. *You really are a bastard, you know that?* he told himself. He was smiling on the inside, from ear to ear. There the man lay, slack-jawed, one arm dangling off the bed, head of thick white hair gleaming like a pearl in the sunlight that filtered in from the room's open shutters.

"I see you really were his friend," the old woman said. "I can see it in your eyes."

"Uh, well...we went through a lot, Tolvan and me."

She nodded. "Go ahead, take a moment with him. I'll just be out in the garden."

The old woman left from a back door. Heren listened to her footfalls fade. He stuck a loaf of old bread in his satchel for the road, then drew out his saw and started cutting.

There were plenty of things Heren wasn't proud of. Stealing the head off a dead man was the least of them. *He doesn't need it anymore, does he?* Still, he left the old woman a pile of silver bits; more than that old Tolvan had ever managed, he reckoned. He left town at a gallop.

A landscape of farmland and pastures rolled by as he crossed Pellon's interior toward Old Crown and the coast. He'd been born in this sort of country, though he'd never wanted anything but to leave it. He snorted a laugh at the thought. Life in the army had taught him the value of a peaceful existence, sure, now that it was well out of reach.

"Unless I pull this off."

He found the kind of man he needed at a wharf-side tavern in Old Crown. The city was half the size of the capital, Paellia, but just as foul in the underparts. Smugglers of all sorts, mercenaries, loan-sharks and every other kind of predator fed off the working folk. Manacles hanging from the man's belt marked him a bounty-hunter as clear as a signpost.

Heren slid onto the stool next to him and leaned close enough to make the man flinch. "You ever heard of a ball-scratch by the name of Iron-Top?"

The bounty hunter looked at him, blinked, then tried to take a casual sip of his brew. "Can't say I have."

Heren smiled. "Let's not waste each other's time, you and I. Got a proposition that just might make you a nice sum of coin, if you're interested. And I know a bounty-hunter is always interested."

Heren talked and the man listened. It was pretty straightforward. Using Tolvan's head—bloating and misshapen now anyway—along with Heren's well-recognized sword, the man would claim to have killed the infamous Iron-Top. He could take his pick from the bounties and collect a fortune. Easiest shine a man ever made.

"It's free gold, right in your lap," Heren told him. "All you have to do is live up to your end."

"And you?"

"Don't you worry about me. Just meet me out back of this tavern after dark to make the hand-off. You can take my sword now, a token of good faith."

Heren whistled as he walked, headed for the little campsite beyond the city walls where he'd stowed Tolvan's head. He made only one stop along the way, haggling a price for passage on a vessel leaving the docks the next morning. The ship was headed east and south, to the distant Kingdom of Rath. *Wonder what it's like,* he mused. He'd heard it was warm year around.

A half-moon bathed the alley behind the Gray Gander in pale stripes, interspersed by deep shadow, when he arrived for the hand-off. The bounty hunter was already there. He leaned up against a wall, seemingly at ease, but Heren knew an ambush when he saw one.

"Here's old Iron-Top," the bounty hunter said, all smiles. "Ready to disappear?"

Heren ignored that. He heaved a sigh, waited for the two other men to materialize from the darkness behind him. Tolvan's head hung in a bag from his grip. It would have to do.

The bounty hunter let his manacles fall loose from one hand with an ominous jangle. "Seems you've guessed what's going on here. Well, it's true, the game's up. Put your hands out, and let's do this the easy way, Iron-Top."

Heren heard one of the men behind him swear, but he never took his eye off the bounty hunter. "Why though? Why share the profits?"

"Why?" The man snorted a laugh. "Did some asking around. Turns out there's more to be made bringing you in alive. A lot more."

Heren had a feeling he knew how it had gone. "You splitting three ways then?" He half-turned, the question aimed at the men behind him. By the look on the face of the closer one, a narrow-eyed bastard with a sword held low and ready, that wasn't the deal.

"Hired muscle." Heren shook his head. "Nothing more. And I bet they didn't even know what they were walking—"

He swung Tolvan's head mid-sentence, caught Narrow-eyes across the face, sent him stumbling to the pavers. Heren let the momentum of that swing carry him through, toward the alley wall. The second tough lurched forward, stabbed at Heren's gut, but he dropped the head and its sack to swat the blade aside, stepping in, grabbing the man from the side in a bear hug. The bounty hunter had drawn and started forward, but Heren turned with the bastard in his arms, used him as a shield to meet the oncoming thrust.

The hired tough took the blade in the side, and Heren shoved him into the bounty hunter. He sidestepped, Heren, snatched up the sack again, swung viciously to send the bounty hunter crashing face-first into the back wall of the inn. The man hit with a grunt, dropping his weapon, slid down to the ground, rolled to find the notorious Iron-Top standing over him with his own sword leveled at his throat.

"Wait—"

Heren didn't. What was the point? He cut the man's throat and let him gurgle out his last breath. Behind him, the narrow-eyed tough had only just begun to rise.

Heren was on him in a second.

"Go ahead," the man said. "Get it over with."

Heren lined his sword up with the grizzled stubble on the man's neck, but paused. The white tabard of a Paellian soldier peeked out from under his cloak.

A flicker of hope crossed the man's face. "Just doing it for the silver," he said, "if that means anything. Wouldn't have dared if I knew it was you, Captain. You can bet I would have run in the other direction."

"Man your age should have some wisdom," Heren agreed.

"If I did, I wouldn't have listened to that goat-humping bounty hunter in the first place. I'd be at the barracks, happy to collect my pay and stand at my post."

"But you needed some copper for wine, was it? Or was it some woman got you into this?"

"Ha! It's my ass. Well, my hip really. I can't take it anymore, hurts all day and all night. I needed this score to get me out. Man can't get a break in the soldier's life though, can he."

"A break?" Heren snorted. The sun was down, but some measure of warmth must've stuck to the old snake. He lowered his sword a hair.

"You might be the luckiest man alive," Heren said. "The one and only to cross this bastard and leave with a profit."

The old soldier was looking plenty hopeful now, eyes all round. "That right?"

Heren nodded, "In this bag here is the head of old Iron-Top. You understand me?"

The man blinked. "I daresay it is. What do you know?"

"And that sword there?" Heren pointed to the sheathed weapon at the dead bounty hunter's waist. "That's his sword if anyone needs further proof. You killed him. He was getting old anyway. Your friends didn't make it, so you'll have to keep the bounty for yourself."

The old soldier nodded, licked his lips. He didn't look like he really believed his luck until Heren tucked the blade in his hand away, at his side, behind his belt.

"Old Iron-Top, finally dead," the man said with a shaky laugh. "Dead, by all the gods! And that's the truth. Won't anyone have to go looking for the likes of him again, I reckon."

Heren nodded. He had some wit, the old man. *Even if he can't fight worth a damn.*

Heren turned to stoop over the other tough, stripped the scabbard off his belt, sheathed the weapon proper. Extending a hand, he helped the old soldier to his feet. "The gods love you, brother. Don't spit on the gift they've just given you."

There were still a few hours before the ship to Rath was schedule to depart. Heren strode the pre-dawn streets of Old Crown feeling a new man. *Warm all year round, good for the joints.* It was a sworn realm of course, there would be Paellians from time to time, but if they thought old Iron-Top was dead, maybe they wouldn't find what they weren't looking for.

It all depended on whether the old soldier kept up his end, of course. But why wouldn't he? Heren stopped in the middle of the street, across from a brothel where a thin young prostitute and an even thinner old one tried to wave him over. He smiled and turned their way.

"Need a tumble, old bull?" the young one purred.

"Not today ladies, fine as you both look. I just wanted to see if you had something else for an old bull, as you call him."

The younger woman smiled but the older one frowned.

"No need to fret, miss, just looking for some dye. The kind a woman might use on her hair?"

"Well, I think that downy white is sexy," said the younger one. "Besides, I've got the thing to make you feel young again right here." She ran a hand along her curves, right down to her crotch.

"I've got your dye," the older woman put in. Now she was smiling. "And for a few extra, I'll set it for ya' too. No one will even recognize you when you walk out of this place, mark my words."

Iron-Top matched her smile. "That's what I'm after."

Author's Note

This story just came out of the blue. The concept of an aging warrior wanting out isn't a new one, but I felt like a retelling of the trope presented a perfect canvas to paint a few fight scenes on.

If you liked the action sequences of Iron and Snow, you might enjoy my debut series, DOG OF WAR. If you don't like waiting, join my newsletter for another action-packed story at www.deankastle.com. In addition to this freebie, other bonus content, and special offers, you'll be the first to know when projects like DOG OF WAR land.

Cheers!

-DK

BAD-LEG

E aric sat in a row beside the other criminals, waiting for his turn to die. Down the tunnel, beyond the door of iron bars, a man in rich woolens stood in the center of the fighting space, shouting up at spectators crowded on wooden benches that seemed to lean over the edge of the pit. The people cheered and shouted back.

The man's voice trailed off, replaced by the baying of hounds. And then growls, whines, and about the most vicious animal sounds Earic had ever heard.

"I just want it to be over," an oldster that stunk of spirits said from Earic's left. "I just want it to be over."

From Earic's right a smaller voice piped up. "I don't."

He was a young one, the lad on his right. Earic couldn't help feeling a little sorry for what the boy faced. But judging by the yipes and whines echoing down the tunnel, it was the beast in the arena he should have felt sorry for at that moment. He didn't feel sorry for himself.

"It'll be over soon enough," he said, and leaned back against the cold stones. His leg ached, from the hip right down to the knee. At least that would end soon. So too the shame, the guilt, the voices of the dead, asking how he yet lived, why he'd run instead of joining them in the dust.

Two men in armor came laughing down the tunnel and Earic blinked, came back to the present. He realized the baying of the hounds had faded to the odd growl, a snarl or two. The first of the day's events was done. He snorted. The blood-hungry spectators had whet their appetites, but no doubt they wanted more.

And these two men would give it to them.

Well, Earic mused, *they'd give them something.*

Neither of them stood as high as Earic's navel—dwarfs, the both of them—and by the casual chatter and occasional grin, he reckoned they wouldn't be killing one another either.

"Bloody Paellians," Earic cursed. They called his folk in Turia brutish and crude, while the wealthiest among the southern folk slipped away to arenas like this one here in Adamar to sip spirits and watch other men die.

The two armored dwarfs tottered out, banged each other around a bit, and tottered back inside the tunnel, replaced by two women, a black-skinned Southerner and a tilt-eyed Dragonlander. As with the men before them, they swung their weapons around a bit, but both came out alive.

"Can't be much longer," Earic said. Voices from down the tunnel confirmed it.

"...make it worth their while," a man in finery was saying, the same one who'd addressed the crowd earlier. "I remind you; our patrons have paid good silver for this."

A hefty man, cloaked in luxuriant fur answered. "My men know their job."

A pig in pearls, that one, Earic reckoned, judging by the once-broken nose, the heavy shoulders. But the other man had reached the front of the line, up near the entrance to the fighting ground. He cleared his throat, his address aimed at the condemned this time.

"You aren't here because of your virtues, my friends. You aren't here because of a shining light within you. You're here as punishment for your crimes. Murder, robbery, assault, rape. Heinous crimes, one and all.

"But the gods can be merciful. All men err, do they not? Do they not deserve a chance to redeem themselves? Have the gods not told us as much time and time again in their Omnibus? Well, men, by the grace of the wise Prince Neurian, you too shall have a chance to redeem yourself. A chance to win back the favor of the gods. A chance to *live*."

Earic would have laughed if there was any trace of joy left in him. "Never heard so much donkey shit," he muttered.

Fancy-cloak frowned, looked down the line for who'd said it. He started talking again but Earic wasn't listening. He closed his eyes, his mind gone to Lord Merold and his boy, Lane. *Food for worms now.* The Lord had been a good man, and his son, still just a child, his life cut short before it had really begun. A pain in the chest screwed up Earic's face, an ache worse than the throb in his bad leg. He should have died with those two—and all the rest—not here, with the drunkard to his left, the young stranger to his right.

Earic blinked, came back to the present as guards in Adamar's blue cloaks pulled them to their feet. The pain shot through his leg, right to the base of his skull. He winced, rubbed at his thigh best he could in manacles. The iron gate creaked open and a push got the line hobbling toward the fighting ground. At the entrance, another pair of guards unshackled each man's wrists and ankles. As the first in line stepped out of the tunnel, a vile, hateful noise of jeers and curses rained down. They were criminals after all, convicted men, sentenced to death—Earic as well.

A third guardsman handed out rusty weapons, chinked swords, and dull axes. He mouthed half-hearted words of encouragement and the gate closed behind them. Earic looked at the rabble huddled there by the closed iron door. Sword-fodder if ever he'd seen it, worse than the farmhands and shepherds the lords sometimes scraped together under their war-banners. At least those men believed they deserved to live.

A trumpet sounded. Earic took the cue. Bare feet crunched on fine gravel as he limped out into the space. He looked up at the sneering faces above, turned a half circle, bathed in the spittle and insults that rained down. He was ready.

Still, he couldn't stop his warrior's eye from studying the fighting ground, one of the famous pits of Adamar. It wasn't more than ten yards across. And there couldn't have been a hundred men and women in the stands, however fine the embroidery of their cloaks, the gleam of their goblets. He noted three more doors into the pit, two of them solid, built of the same wood as the rough-hewn walls, stained dark in places, freshly splattered with gore in others. Damp patches of gravel marked the excrement and blood where man or beast had died. Furrows in the gravel betrayed the path of the bodies that had been dragged out.

At least in a space this size, it wouldn't take long, Earic supposed. He looked across to the third entrance, a miniature portcullis of iron like the door they'd come in from. Movement caught his eye through the bars. It swung open on creaky hinges and three men with swords and round shields prowled out.

A great roar from the crowd greeted them. The first wore a horned helm, a heavy looking thing that had to give him an aching neck. The helmet of the second was more practical, with a closed faceguard hiding his features, the kind that would limit your sight, even if you'd be thankful for it in a shield wall. The last of the pit-fighters wore no helmet at all, his head shaved bald, a red eye-patch stretched over his disfigured face.

They turned circles, raised blades, beat them against their shields, pumped their fists. The crowd cheered even more.

"Thram's hairy balls, get on with it!" Earic cursed. He stood at the front of the eight cowering men, weapon down at his side, waiting. But like cats playing with mice, the three fighters—the *execution-ers*—came forward at a leisurely pace, weapons raised half-hearted-ly, corralling the condemned men into a whimpering knot near the locked gate they'd just come through.

More like dogs herding sheep, Earic corrected himself. *Wolves, actu-ally, playing at being dogs.*

If the men behind him had known anything of war, they would have refused to be herded. They would have fallen on the three exe-cutioners at the mouth of the tunnel, hemmed them in, cut them to ribbons. Instead, they cowered at the far end, waiting for the slaughter.

The clang of weapons turned his head as the man with the horned helm aimed a lackadaisical swing at the drunkard. The poor bastard shrieked but managed a parry. With that, the rest of the condemned men bolted in every direction. The crowd hooted and jeered. The other two executioners went after marks of their own.

Laughing executioners chased running criminals, herded them into one another, and the first one died with a piteous cry. Earic didn't run. He couldn't have with that leg. Eventually, the man with the eyepatch prowled toward him, the tip of his sword dragged behind him through the gravel, an evil grin across his face.

"Ready to die, Bad-Leg?"

Earic tilted his face heavenward, closed his eyes. But the blow didn't come.

"Fight, you idiot!" Eyepatch hissed. "These rich bastards didn't pay to see lambs bled."

"Just kill me, bastard," Earic said.

His eyes were still closed, but stars shot across them, under his eyelids, and his head rocked back. The pain hit him a split second later and his bed leg went out from under him. He landed on his side with a grunt.

Rolling to his back, Earic gazed up, waited for the grey sky above to fade to black, but after a moment he realized he'd only been punched. The clatter of weapons rang in his ear, the screams of dying men, the cheers of the crowd. His face throbbed as blood pumped through his swollen cheekbone, but the pain of it quickened his pulse, tightened his fist on the haft of the weapon in his hands.

He looked down. It was an ill-weighted axe. He croaked a laugh. He didn't intend to use it anyway. He deserved to die; that's why he'd picked that fight that landed him in jail in the first place. But it seemed he'd have to work a little harder for it.

And that axe felt good in his hands. His eyes closed and he saw Merold's face as the blade emerged red through his stomach, thrust in from the back. He saw Lane hacked down to one knee, dispatched with a second chop, stabbed with a third. He felt the mace against his leg again, the stones against his face, his back as he tumbled downhill into cold, fast running water. A hand went to his chest as he remembered coughing his lungs out on a muddy bank downstream. That pain clenched his heart again.

Earic shook it off and pushed up to his feet. There were dead men on the ground, dying men, moaning their last breaths. He turned, looking for Eyepatch, spied him trading blows with the young criminal from his right, the lad giving it his all despite an obvious lack of training.

"Ha!" The executioner laughed. "Yes!"

They traded blows, the boy gaining confidence, driving Eyepatch back. Then, just as the lad brought his sword forward for a killing thrust, the executioner sidestepped, stuck out a leg to trip the young criminal, and ran him through as he hit the ground.

"Ha!" The smug bastard rested a hand on his belly as he laughed. Earic felt the lump rising on the side of his face where he'd been hit. He felt something else too, in his chest. It wasn't just pain though. It was fury.

"Whoreson bastard!" Before he'd really thought about it, he'd thrown his axe. He didn't get the rotation right—how could he with the pitiful balance of the thing—but by luck, it hit Eyepatch head-first, like a javelin.

"Ooof!" he grunted, covered his chest after the fact. Earic was already limping toward him, sword snatched up off the gravel along the way.

But Horn-helm stepped in the way. "Here's one with some life—"

A savage swing at the face cut the executioner short. He deflected the blow with a raised shield, but Earic used the force on his rebounded blade to send a cut at the bastard's thigh. It sliced just below the hem of Horn-helm's protective leathers, scored a deep red line. The executioner swore, tried to backpedal, stumbled, fell on top of his shield on his left side. He swung with the blade in his right hand to keep Earic back, but he hadn't charged in for the killing blow. He couldn't have, not with that bad leg.

Instead, he chopped down viciously, mangled the executioner's exposed ankle.

"Ahhhh!"

He was down. Earic left him there. He turned back toward Eyepatch, but it was the man with the closed faceguard that came barreling toward him, sword raised. Earic stepped into the swing as he came, caught the blade with his own, up high, took the brunt of the charge against his chest. The force bowled him right over, but not before he hooked Faceguard's leg with his own, dragging him down alongside.

The gravel knocked the wind out of him as he hit, but by some luck, the executioner's helm came right off, leaving his face exposed, and sending the man's mouth right into Earic's chin. Pain shot up into Earic's jaw as a tooth or something else gouged him, but the now-helmless fighter got the worst of it. He howled, rolling off Earic to one side, one hand on his mouth.

Earic rolled in the other direction, sucked in air, clutched at his gut. He dragged himself to one knee. Something roared in his ears.

The crowd. *Blood-thirsty bastards.* Earic grabbed a handful of gravel, pushed to both feet. He squared up his enemy—a pink-faced swine—hobbled forward on his bad leg, swung with all the hatred he had.

Once, twice, the executioner parried. With his left hand, Earic threw that handful of gravel at the man's face, let him flail, blind for the moment, where he thought Earic would be. Then Earic tossed his sword from right hand to left, stretched forward as far as he could go with a stab at the man's middle.

The blow found flesh. Earic let loose the hilt as it stuck in his enemy's stomach, dropped sideways to the gravel as a backhand swing came at him. The blade nicked his arm, drew blood, but it was the executioner who staggered backward, collapsed to one knee, pulled the rusty sword from his stomach to release a fountain of blood. With a groan, he crumpled, glassy eyes staring past Earic, through the gates to Vorda's cold hell.

Earic turned, panting, searching for Eyepatch. Dead men littered the ground, facedown or curled around their wounds. The world shook with the noise of the spectators' shouts, the banging of their hands against timber. They leaned from the first rows of seats over the edge of the enclosure to pound the walls of the pit.

"Fight! Fight! Fight!"

Across the killing ground, staring daggers at him from under his brow, a single furious eye locked with Earic's.

"Bloody bastard." Earic spit. He bent, stripped the sword from one executioner and started warily toward another.

"Got some fight, have ya?" Eyepatch said, circling slowly.

"More than you can handle."

Earic said no more. He skipped forward, getting used to fighting on his bad leg now, and sent a resounding blow sideways at Eyepatch. The executioner took it on his shield, replied with a straight, business-like thrust. Earic twisted, let it slide past, and they parted again. The crowd howled for joy.

But Earic was at a heavy disadvantage and he knew it. With that shield to protect his left and his sword in his right, Eyepatch could stop an attack and counter with his own faster than Earic could. As they circled, he searched for a weakness, something to exploit. Thank the gods this fool had been slaughtering lambs so long he'd forgotten what it was to lock jaws with another wolf. He came on slow, dragging things out, by habit maybe, allowing Earic enough time to think.

The eye. Of course!

A mad giggle escaped Earic's lips, and he tossed his sword from right hand to left, started toward Eyepatch's blind side. Earic wasn't as good with his left, but he wasn't half-bad either. And coming at the executioner's sword arm allowed the bastard less opportunity to counter from the other side, except with a swipe of the shield, an obtuse, unwieldy proposition.

Earic hammered at Eyepatch—high, low, straight, arcing—praying all the while the weapon in his grip didn't shatter. The pit-fighter grunted but met each strike with a firm parry and the occasional riposte despite the attack at his impaired side. Tilting his head, apparently, was all he needed to see Earic's attacks.

"That all you got?" Eyepatch sneered. With a lunge, he backed Earic up, then raised his shield and drove at his bad right leg, sending him into a frantic retreat. A heel clipped something and Earic went over backwards. Years in the sword-yard taught him how to land with a roll, a motion he continued until he was well out of Eyepatch's reach.

The crowd roared. If he'd imagined the place was shaking before, Earic was sure of it now.

But Eyepatch was barreling toward him again. Coming up to one knee just in time, Earic caught a ferocious overhand chop with one hand at the hilt, the other on the flat of his blade. The force of it rattled him from his wrists to his teeth, and the poor weapon bent, but it took Eyepatch off balance too. Earic dropped it, lunged forward to wrap the executioner around the knees in a wrestler's tackle, sweeping him to the ground.

Fists, elbows, teeth, nails. Blows missed or landed, curses flew alongside spittle and blood. Earic ripped the patch off his enemy, clawed at the slimy hole in his skull. Eyepatch sent a headbutt back into Earic's face and he saw stars for a second time. They rolled one way and the next until they were up against something—a corpse—and Earic got caught on the bottom. A forearm pressed against his throat. He dug at good eye and empty socket alike, felt blood or slobber drip onto his face, but his arms started to go weak. The light faded. He heard something like a squawk from Eyepatch as the world went black

A pounding against the timbers of the arena matched the pounding in Earic's head as he opened his eyes. He blinked. It had only been moments, he reckoned, but Eyepatch was off him. A strong grip at either side pulled him to his feet, a pair of guardsmen in the blue cloaks of Adamar. They walked him in a limping circle around the edge of the fighting ground.

"Raise a fist," one of the guards said out of the side of his mouth.

Earic tried to make sense of those words. He looked up, saw the faces staring down. Their rhythmic chant reached him. "Bad-Leg! Bad-Leg! Bad-Leg! Bad-Leg!"

He looked down to his feet, saw them move—step, drag, step, drag—as if by themselves. He raised a weary hand, then extended a curled forefinger, palm turned up. A finger up the ass for one and all of them.

The crowd hooted even louder. One of the guardsmen chuckled. "You tell 'em, Bad-Leg."

They started toward the tunnel with the portcullis door, but Earic pulled them to a stop. "Wait."

A slim, bronze-skinned man had begun dragging bodies out. Earic limped past him toward the young criminal, on his side on the gravel. He didn't have to kneel to see the lad had bled out, future cut short, just like young Lane. A sigh escaped Earic's lips, and his exhaustion caught up with him. He would have cried if he had the strength. He would have crumpled to the ground if his leg hadn't locked up straight.

In the tunnel, they laid him out on a stretcher. He stared at the curved stone ceiling, thinking of Merold and Lane and the rest, wondering how in all hell he still wasn't dead. An angry voice from down the tunnel grew louder until it was right over him. Earic couldn't have cared less.

"...bloody convict killed one of my lads! Ruined another! I demand his head! Do you know how much that cost me?"

A second voice answered, the man in the rich woolens who'd addressed the crowd. "This man is the property of the arena. If you ever want your fighters in this institution again, you'll calm yourself."

"He—"

"Gods above and below, this isn't your first game! You knew the risk!"

Earic finally turned his head enough to see it was the pig in pearls arguing with the arena's announcer. A pair of guardsmen eyed Piggie warily. It looked like they might have to step in, until a set of approaching footfalls turned attention down the tunnel.

"Now that was something to see," the new arrival said, a stocky man with steel-grey hair and beard, both trimmed short.

"Here's the old crow," Pig-in-pearls said. "Always quick to arrive at the scene of a slaughter."

"Slaughter's your business, not mine. But I'll have a word with the director if he'll bend an ear."

"Will you now?" Piggie rested hands on hips. "Want this lout for your academy, eh? Ha! Look at him. He can barely walk. Look at all the blood! He might be dead already."

Earic wasn't dead. Not yet, even if that's what he'd come for. The three men cursed each other and clucked back and forth until another man, the bronze-skinned corpse-dragger, arrived to kneel over Earic, eyes narrowed.

"Let's see what the healer has to say," one of the men muttered.

"Healer?" Earic croaked. He couldn't help but laugh. The bronze-skinned man met his eye, started chuckling in answer. That revealed a set of perfect white teeth. There was something scary about those choppers. Or maybe it was just the fact that the man they called 'healer' was the same man that hauled away the bodies.

"He'll never fight again," Piggie was saying. "Just give me his head. Your clients have gotten their money's worth already."

"Well?" said the announcer, the one Steel-grey had called 'the director.' He looked to the healer. The bronze-skinned man nodded, rested a hand on Earic's neck, closed his eyes.

Earic couldn't say exactly what he felt, something like a shiver up his spine. But it didn't hurt. And when this 'healer' opened his eyes, he flashed those teeth again in another smile.

Gods all be damned, but he was a scary sonofabitch.

"He'll live."

"But his leg—"

"He fights well enough on one leg," Steel-grey said. "The question is, does he want to?" His eyes went down, met Earic's. "Do you want to fight, son? Do you want to live?"

Earic didn't answer, just lifted his chin, looked away. He heard a noise, turned his neck to find Steel-grey had kneeled next to him.

"Been at this a long time, son. Long enough to know when a man's come here with one end in mind. I see that right here in this tunnel. But that's not what I saw out there in the pit."

Earic mumbled a curse but refused to meet the man's eye.

"You came here to die, seems like. But you've still got a lot of fight in you. Isn't that right?"

Earic met his gaze finally. "And why should I fight? It's easier to die. And it's what I got coming."

Steel-grey shook his head. "We all got it coming eventually, don't we? But there'll be more boys like that dead one out there today, Bad-Leg. More young lads who haven't got a chance. A man like you, maybe you could teach some of them. Maybe you could keep some of them alive."

"So *that's* what you're after," Piggie said from over Steel-grey's shoulder.

Earic didn't say anything. But Steel-grey nodded as if he had. "Maybe you deserve to die, just like you said. I don't know. But those youngsters, they might deserve a chance."

"Maybe," Earic muttered.

"That's right. A chance against the likes of One-eye and all the rest. You may have taken two of those killers out of the game, but there's more where they came from. And there's still One-eye."

Earic fell silent. He thought of Merold and Lane, prayed for their forgiveness.

"What do you say? I get the feeling maybe you *do* want to live, eh Bad-Leg?"

"One-eye." Earic repeated.

Steel-grey nodded. "I bet you wouldn't mind another crack at that nut, eh?"

Earic met his gaze for a good long moment. He licked his lips, tasted blood, and spit.

Author's Note

Gladiators—I just had to! In my debut series, DOG OF WAR, the protagonist's history as a pit-fighter is mentioned from the very first chapter as well. This was always something I wanted to explore. As I wrote DOG OF WAR, the story of Adamar's gladiatorial arenas cried out to be told.

The character Bad-Leg is just one of many slated to hit the page in another series currently slow-burning in the background. I won't say anything more about that just yet, but if you liked what you read and want to know when the next project releases, join my newsletter at www.deankastle.com. In addition to periodic updates, bonus content, and more, you'll receive another free story.

Hope you enjoyed this!

-DK

SWORD-DAUGHTER

A red sun sank behind hills of snow-matted pines when the messenger arrived. Vriana watched his fingers twitch at the hem of his leathers and she knew. Her father was dead.

The man confirmed it in solemn tones. She didn't speak, just stared at the goat roasting over the fire, skin crackling, fat bubbling. So many things she'd meant to tell her father, so many things she'd tried to show him.

"Did you hear me?"

Vriana blinked, looked up at the messenger. She drew a knife from the back of her belt and the man stepped back. One of Viro's men. She cut a strip of meat from the carcass roasting over the fire in front of her. "Tell my brother I am coming."

The messenger tramped back the way he'd come, across the packed snow, between the maze of hide tents to his shaggy horse, and back out into the blustery cold. He was a dedicated man, brave too, but a fool to ride the frozen miles of Ilia in winter and at night.

But he feared to stay among this band of outcasts. The stories of their plunders were legion. Their crimes too.

Fryngaer arrived, dark hair hanging in perfect waves down his back. "Is it true?"

"He is dead."

Fryngaer eyed her with sympathy. He lifted a hand toward her then pulled it back to his side, thinking better of it. Vriana was glad for that. Not here, not in front of her warriors. There would be time for sympathy later, for a tender touch or angry sex, whatever she felt. But there was never a time to show weakness.

"Ready the band," she told him. "We travel at dawn."

"To Ehken Laer?"

"Do you think I would miss my father's funeral?"

Fryngaer frowned. "It might be easier if you did."

"Easier for Viro maybe. But I do not care what's easy for him."

"I just don't want you to do anything foolish. In front of all the tribe. He'll use that against you, use it to cheat you."

"It will be even easier for him to cheat me if I don't show my face."

"Vriana—"

"You are a man for peace, Fryngaer. But in order to avoid a fight, sometimes you must first invite it."

Fryngaer smiled. "It seems like we're forever inviting fights, this band of ours. And not once have we managed to avoid it."

"You don't know Viro like I do." She rested a hand on his shoulder. "He's my brother. We're family."

The timber-walled hillfort of Laer sat silent under its mantle of snow. A few leather and fur-clad tribesmen hailed Vriana with smiles as she crossed through the gates, up gravel-strewn tracks toward the steep-roofed hall at the peak. But most stayed to their longhouses at this time of year. They had no reason to be about. Or perhaps they feared her too.

Halfway up she saw the remains of the pyre, a black mar on the white scene and she realized Father was already ash. Her feet stopped all on their own. Anger boiled up in her, her hands shook at her side. She balled them into fist—to stop them trembling though, not to fight. A deep breath of the frigid forest air cooled her head. She checked her emotions, shoved them down, mastered them. To come storming after her brother would only prove that she was just another frivolous woman, like he'd always said.

But she'd held her tears for so long, all the many miles from the border with Thiringia to the great hillfort at the heart of Laer, by the river and meadow. Here was the place to make public her grief, beat her chest, claw the earth. She arrived in front of the pyre's remains, memory of her father's hand around hers as she first gripped the reins, his beard scratching her neck, the smell of his skin. She sank to her knees and screamed.

Her warriors took the cue, crowded behind her, not less than a hundred and twenty men, a handful of women too. They pounded their shields, howled, hugged one another fiercely, tore at their beards. Vather the Great, Govendi Lonegas of the Laer tribe was gone. So what if many of them had been cast out by him, stripped of honors? He was the father of their mistress, Princess Vriana. If it was a sad day for her, together they grieved.

"Sister," a voice called.

Vriana looked up through blurry eyes. Viro stood across the crumbling black remains. It had been over a year, but he hadn't changed, except that his beard was cut short, a sign of grief. The same thick auburn hair as her own hung down to his shoulders, on his left hip he wore a sword, just as she did. But on his right hung the antler-horned, emerald encrusted hilt of Theka, ancestral heirloom of Laer's kings.

How Vriana wanted to stab the tip of that dagger into her brother's foot.

She pushed up to her feet, lifted her chin. "You couldn't wait for me? You had to set the fires before I arrived?"

"I...didn't think you were coming."

"Didn't think, or didn't want?"

"Vriana—"

"I told the messenger I was coming."

"Yes, but—"

"You think so little of me?"

"Maybe I thought it would have been better if you didn't come."

Vriana sucked in a long breath of cold air, stared at the ash-blackened snow beneath her, dug her fingernails into her palm. She wrestled her rage down, subdued it, then turned to wave at Fryngaer.

"The gifts."

Ornate quilts, staffs inlaid with carved yellow tusks, knives, arrows and weapons of all kinds tumbled down as each of her band made an offering. Fryngaer piled them neatly beside the cold, crumbling ash mound that had been her father's pyre, her father himself. Vriana didn't miss the wide-eyes of the on-lookers. Rich gifts, these.

She called for fire and oil. "Light of the Maker shepherd you to the place of rest and green hills."

Fryngaer doused the offerings, sprinkling hickory shavings for scent, and handed Vriana a burning brand. She set it all alight. Smoke swirled around them, rose to the grey skies.

Her warriors stood with straight backs, once-shamed men, orphans, freed slaves, whores, all of them turned fighters now. Vriana led them, sipping dark, heady Eyfra from her flask, pouring a measure of the liquor down to feed the flames. Her band followed suit, all who had drink to give. The fire roiled, lashed at the grey skies like angry red whips.

Vriana didn't drink that night, though others drank freely. Viro provided the feast, as was his obligation. They'd traveled far, after all, and he was their chieftain now.

Vriana watched her band eat and drink, scattered on pelts, cross-legged, throughout the hall. Her hand touched the pouch of silver and gold ingots at her waist. Viro would receive his tithe as he deserved, but no more. In the morning, they would return to the borderlands.

When the prayers were all sung, the meat and drink passed, she left Fryngaer to find her brother. The central hearth blazed bright, threw welcome heat and orange light off the high rafters, the sawed tree rings, the fur-clad warriors snoozing or talking softly in twos and threes. She found Viro at the back of the hall behind a hide screen in his personal chamber.

He eyed her approach, nestled among his furs beside a glowing brazier, cup in hand. He drained it and refilled it from a bulging skin, drunk already if the pink in his cheeks was any indication.

"Your men look well," he said, tossing the skin over.

Vriana snatched it out of the air, filled her cup halfway and sat across from him. "I come to pay the tithe."

Viro watched her warily.

"You are chieftain now, aren't you? Did you think I wouldn't honor that?"

"I never know what you'll do."

Vriana laughed that off, took a sip from her cup. It was throat-burning Eyfra her brother had been drinking, not berry-wine. She winced, set the cup down.

"We could be good for each other, you and I, brother. There's a reason the Thirings haven't troubled you these past years. A reason you've been able to cultivate the roots, multiply the herds. It's because *I've* been troubling *them*."

"And you've profited from that I gather."

"As I should. I've lost men too. But you know how I love a good fight." She forced a smile.

Her brother only frowned. "I know you did when we were children. I didn't think you'd keep on with it."

"Did you think I'd stow my sword away and take up weaving?"

"I thought you'd marry. I didn't think you'd gather every lone wolf out of these hills and march them off to nip at the heels of our neighbors."

"They're not lone wolves anymore, brother. They stand proud now. And they've done more than nip at the heels."

Viro sighed.

"What? Speak your thoughts, don't make noises like a goat."

"Vriana, these are dangerous men." Viro sat forward. "Desperate men. Why else would they fall in under a woman?"

Vriana didn't even bristle. Such was the way of the forest, of the world, as far as she'd heard. She looked down into the cup in her hand, chose her words.

"I didn't come here to argue, Viro. I came here to pay your tithe. You are chieftain now. Govendi of the tribe. You are the son."

"And you are the daughter. Your actions reflect on me, Vriana."

"What is it you blame me for now, Viro?"

"That massacre down south. Did you have to mutilate the bodies? Couldn't you just take what you wanted and leave?"

"I may not have buried those bastards, but when I left them, they were whole."

"You deny it now? You never denied it before."

"Why would I? Let people fear me."

"They're calling you an animal, a froth-mouth she-wolf at the head of a pack of mangy dogs."

Vriana took a pull from her cup then, breathed to calm herself. "Are you too weak to claim me, brother? Even now that you are chieftain? Too weak even to let me stand by your side?"

"I—"

"It must have been thieves that hacked up those Thirings, because it wasn't me. Out of the Sunlands. If that's what's got you scared."

"I am not a child anymore, Vriana. I am not scared. But you keep those filthy butchers out of Ehken Laer. Pay your tithe and take them. I never want to see their cursed hides in this hall again."

"Fine. But watch how you speak of my band. If there were shamed men among them, they've redeemed themselves now. If there was a criminal in my midst, I've killed him already. They've fought for Laer all these years—"

"They fought for glory and plunder!" Viro snorted. "Not for you or for me. And not for the Laeri."

"Should they not seek glory? Like everyone else? Do your men leave the spoils of war behind them for the crows? Or for Sunlander brigands?"

Her hand trembled. She took a long pull at the liquor, swallowed a curse as it burned a trail down her throat. Still, it calmed her nerves. Things would never change. She didn't hope to change them really, didn't want to even. She just wanted some fraction of the respect she was due.

"Maybe Fryngaer was right," she muttered. She rose, left her brother there in his furs.

It took a good hour, but in one pass, Vriana had collected shares from each of her men, coupled them with her own, and returned with Viro's tithe.

"It's all there," she told her brother. "More than you're expecting too, I think." She tossed the leather bag full of ingots down to her brother, still nestled in furs beside his brazier, drink in hand.

"It's not easy being chieftain," he said, not bothering to look inside. "Do you know that?"

Vriana nodded. "I miss him too. It was Father who taught me to ride you know. I remember him wrapping me up in a horse blanket and taking me out on Blackfeet when I was practically still a babe.

"But it was you who taught me to fight. How to hold a sword, how to rely on speed and tricks instead of strength. You used to be so proud. I was the brother you never had."

Viro looked up, eyes solemn, cast in orange firelight. "He called you sword-daughter." He drained his cup, poured another. "He loved you. He really did. And you've done well. Certainly lived up to the name."

"He loved you too."

Viro paused. His expression twisted up and Vriana saw something she'd never seen before: jealousy. He held his tongue, but took a long pull at his liquor, grimaced, and drained the cup to the bottom.

Vriana hugged herself. She wanted to reach out, embrace him, rest her head on his shoulder. To hold him close like she had as a child.

Fryngaer had proved a practical partner and a friend, but if there was a man she cared for, however bad he hurt her, it was her brother.

"Why didn't you wait for me?" she said quietly.

Viro stayed silent a long time. "I don't know."

"I told the messenger I was coming."

"I..." Viro looked up. "I guess I didn't want you to come."

"Why?"

Her brother breathed out a sigh. "Because of this."

"Because of what?

"All of this!" His wave encompassed the entire room. "Don't you get it? He loved you more! He always did! Even when you were gone, away south, stealing herds from the Thirings and crossing the river to plunder Arnus. News would reach him, and he'd smile. His sword-daughter had cut again."

"I didn't do it to spite you, Viro. I did it because I had to."

"Had to?"

"The gods made me this way, more apt to fit arrow to bow than needle to thread. More fit to butcher than to make a stew."

Viro winced.

But how could the truth hurt him, her truth? She watched him pour another cup of Eyfra. She took a pull at her own, drained it to the clear bottom.

"Viro—"

"Maybe it would have been better if you hadn't come. There's more glory to be had at the border after all."

"Not come? Damn you, Viro! He was my father too!"

"You left us!" He stood, with some effort, jabbed a finger in her direction. "You!"

"You drove me out!"

"Only because you didn't know your place!"

"And what did you know? Except how to drink yourself stupid and lay with cupbearers!"

"You...you!" A mote of spittle hit Vriana's cheek, they stood so close. Viro's eyes bulged, stinking breath buffeting her. He shook with rage.

"I *what?* Say it! It was I that should have been the son, and you that should be pouring drinks and stitching cloaks!"

She'd gone too far. He came at her with both hands, clutching at her neck. The knife at the small of her back was out in a flash, and without thinking, it slid right into his stomach.

A gasp escaped Vriana's lips. "Viro!"

But her brother only winced, came harder, squeezing at her throat. She clawed at his hands. The world began to dim. She felt down at her brother's waist, drew that red knife out and plunged it in again, higher this time, and to the left.

Viro's eyes still bulged but his mouth dropped open. "You..."

Vriana left the knife there in his chest, stripped his fingers from her neck, pulled herself away. Her brother collapsed among the furs. The ingots she'd given him lay scattering beneath him.

One of Viro's servants peeked around the edge of hide screen and shrieked. Several groggy warriors appeared on her heels. Swords rasped free.

"She-devil!" a bald fighter cursed, his entire head gone red.

But Fryngaer appeared behind him, clutching his arms to his sides from behind in a bear hug. "Wait!" he hissed.

A second warrior took a step in her direction and Vriana tensed to spring, but more of her men rushed in and Viro's people hesitated. Vriana looked down at her brother. One glassy eye stared at the ceiling, the other was closed. His mouth hung open.

"He's dead," she said. She felt a wail, a sob building inside of her. She looked away. *Not now!*

"Killed your own brother," the bald warrior spat. "To rule the tribe. You'll never rule Laer, wench."

"Then who will?" Fryngaer shot back. "Viro had no sons."

"He—"

"The Thirings fear me," Vriana said, finding her voice. "The Arnui too." She lowered it, took one menacing step toward the man, still clasped all the way around by Fryngaer. "You would do well to fear me."

The bald warrior's eyes narrowed, but as he met her stare the truth of her words seemed to set in. He nodded, shook Frynagaer's hold off him. He glared at the long-haired fighter, then sheathed his sword.

He looked down to Viro, back up to Vriana. "Govendis." He dipped his head.

"Vriana Govendis," others repeated, some murmuring, others loud and with pride. One by one they came to honor their new chieftess until only Fryngaer was left.

"Govendis."

Vriana sighed. It came out as a tremble.

"I know you didn't want this Vriana. I know this isn't what you came here for, that you're not a murderer."

She didn't answer. It was done. She was chieftess. Let them think what they wanted so long as they followed her rule.

"Wake the people," she said. "Build another pyre."

"So soon?"

"And gather gifts. Worthy gifts."

"Yes, Chieftess."

She waved Fryngaer away. Her brother still lay there. Wide-eyed. Slack-jawed. Dead.

She knelt, pushed all the ingots to one side and wrapped him in his furs, wiped liquor and blood from him. She touched his face, still warm but lifeless. And she cried.

Author's Note

Vriana, chieftess of the Laeri, features prominently in my debut series, the DOG OF WAR Epic. She's a woman of few words, always holding her cards close to the vest, but I thought it would be fun to get inside her head. Although her fight scene in this piece is brief, and more emotional than physical, she's involved in plenty of scrapes in DOG OF WAR. To get the book, visit www.deankastle.com/books. html .

If you haven't joined the newsletter already, visit www.deankastle .com to be among the first to know when DOG OF WAR and other projects release. A bonus story is yours with the sign-up, along with periodic updates, exclusive content, and more.

-DK

LIVE BY THE SWORD

I t was a terrible dream. Carn was a child again, watching through the window as strange men swarmed the lanes of his town. They howled, spreading fire from roof to thatched roof. Grig, the smith, ran against them with his hammer, but shiny swords came out and they surrounded him, poked and cut him until he fell. Strong arms grabbed Carn as his father pulled him from the window, latched the shutter, and stuffed him in the cellar. He heard a yell and pounding on their front door. A crash followed. His father cried out, mother screamed, and then he woke up.

He blinked, looked up at the sun-dappled leaves of a huge oak above him. He lay on his back, something hard serving as a pillow beneath his neck. He was a grown man again—of course he was—but where exactly was he?

And who was the man snoring softly across the burned-out campfire. Carn sat up, kicked the blanket off him, climbed to his feet.

The man across the fire opened his eyes. "Finally!" He looked relieved. "I thought you'd sleep forever. Thought you might die, if I'm honest."

Carn looked around. "Where are we?"

"The Boundaries, where else?"

"The Boundaries." Carn worked the words around in his mouth. He'd heard his father speak of those lands, the empty territory near the edge of the forests of Ilia, where the wild tribes dwelled.

He must have been making a face because the man across the fire was eying him sideways. "You alright?"

"Well, I'm not sure. I can't remember...anything."

"Like what?"

"Like how I got here. When I left Hatton. Seems like the last thing I recall was when I was a just a kid, living in the town."

The man blinked. "Never you mind all that. I've got you." He cracked a broad smile, thumped his chest. "Leave it all to me."

"And who are you?"

"Oh boy." The man scratched behind his ear, frowned. "Well, I'm Laric. And I'm your best friend."

Laric got them up and moving. It didn't take more than a few minutes to cover the coals of the fire, gather their things. Carn had a shoulder pack full of odds and ends, a bedroll, and blanket. And a sword.

It was a short-bladed length of iron, leather-wrapped grip, plain round knob for a pommel. He held the sheathed weapon in both hands, frowned down at it. Drawing it out, he examined the chinked but well-honed edge, swung it through the air a few times.

"Coming back to you now, I reckon." Laric flashed that smile.

"It's heavier than it looks."

"Gets heavier by the year, but there's nothing for it."

They started walking, due west, Laric talking all the while. He said there might be green-cloaks about, but Carn didn't know why they had to worry about the king's soldiers.

"You really don't remember me?" Laric asked. "How we got to this field, I can understand, but you don't remember anything before that, like the warlock? The cottage?"

Carn shook his head. "I think I remember some wine?"

His friend blew out a sigh. "Alright, well, we were up in the forest, see? And we came across a cottage."

"In Ilia?"

"That's right."

"An Ilar cottage?"

"Yessir. A longhouse, they call 'em. But that's a cottage more or less."

"What were we doing there?"

"Looking for loot, what else?" Laric grinned.

Carn forced a smile, though he couldn't understand why they'd risk a trek into the lands of the tribes just to loot a cottage.

"Actually," Laric was saying, "we came across the warlock first. It's him we followed until he led us to the cottage."

"Hang on," Carn said, raising a finger. "This man was an Ilar?"

Laric nodded.

"And a warlock?"

Another nod.

"How do you know?"

"Because we followed all the way to the cottage, but when we followed him inside, he disappeared."

"And that's where I lost my memory?" Carn asked.

"You went in first. I circled around behind but there was no way in from there. By the time I came back around front and went inside, you were standing there in a trance. And the Ilar was gone."

Carn mulled over those words as they walked, tall grass sliding against his thighs, damp earth squishing underfoot. It had rained recently, which was good, because that was a dry country. Here and there a lone oak or stand of pines dotted the horizon. Otherwise, it was gentle hills of yellow grass as far as the eye could see.

"What were we doing in that cottage anyway?" Carn said finally.

"Looking for loot. I already said that."

"To steal? What for?"

"For Kael. And for food, something to eat or drink. Maybe a woman if we got lucky."

Carn frowned. He may have lost his memories, but he wasn't a child anymore. He didn't like how that sounded, stealing, taking women. He kept those thoughts to himself.

"So, what do we do now? Head back to Hatton?"

"Thram's purple cock, you really did lose it, didn't you?"

Carn didn't answer. The sun sat high in the sky and sweat rolled down his temples. They walked in silence for a while until Laric pulled them up.

"I know you're hungry."

He was. But he'd already looked through the pack he carried. There was nothing to eat inside. He took a drink from his waterskin instead.

"Don't worry, I got you." Laric rummaged through his own pack, pulled out a strip of dried meat wrapped in a cloth and passed it over. "Go ahead, eat it."

"What about you?"

Laric cracked a broad smile. "I said I got you, didn't I?"

Carn tore at the hard strip with his teeth, tentatively at first, then with more vigor as his tongue got the taste of salt on it and his mouth started watering. Laric just stood there grinning at him.

"Don't worry about me." His friend looked off into the distance, westward. "I reckon we'll be able to snag a few trout at the stream. You probably don't remember, but there's a stream up ahead. I'll hook us some dinner there."

Carn slung his pack off and dropped it under a tree when they reached the little watercourse. He bathed while Laric worked a fishing line upstream. They moved up and down the bank, searching for the right spot, but in the end, Laric was only able to catch one measly fish.

"Thram's hairy ass." He licked his fingers once they'd gutted, roasted, and shared the fish, eating with bare hands. "One bloody fish."

"Maybe we should sleep, try again in the morning?" Carn offered. "I remember my father taking me fishing. He said morning was the best time."

Laric shook his head. "There's still Kael though."

"Is that a town?"

"Might as well be. That's where we're headed."

Carn frowned. "I don't follow."

"He's got a nice little set-up, Kael. It's a camp really, more than it's a town. But they've got everything. We can't show up emptyhanded, mind you. We'll need loot, anyway you look at it. Or a lot of bloody fish."

"Then why go back?"

Laric started poking the fire, throwing a few more sticks on until it blazed bright. He sat back, sighed. The sun was down, the skies growing dark, but orange light reflected in his eyes as he looked up at Carn.

"You see, before Kael, there was a man called Barian. He's the man that took the likes of you and me from our villages. He gave us everything we have: a new life, meat, and ale, and women. We have to avoid green-cloaks mind, but otherwise we're as free as the wind. No yokes, no toiling in the fields. Just free!"

"But we can't go back to Barian. Is he dead?"

Laric nodded. "Live by the sword...you know the rest."

He did. Carn's mother had often advised against such a life. He didn't look down, but he felt the weight of the sheathed blade against his thigh.

"How far is it to Hatton?" he asked. "I wouldn't mind seeing some familiar faces. Maybe that would bring it all back."

Laric frowned. "Well, the thing is, it isn't the same."

"My father—"

"I'm sorry, Carn. They're gone. My folks too. But it's alright." Laric raised his hands at the open sky. "We have all this now. We're free!"

Carn blew out a sigh. Laric didn't seem sad though. He hummed under his breath as he cleaned up after their meager meal. Carn nodded to himself. If he was a man now, he supposed his parents might have been dead a long time already.

"I've just got to get my memory back," he muttered.

"You will, by and by. What we've got to worry about now is Kael."

In the morning, they broke camp and started back east again. After a time, Laric turned them north. At the top of a hill, he motioned a halt.

"There's a cabin over the ridge here," he said. "Down in the dell."

"What are we doing here?"

"Loot, remember?"

"Loot." Carn nodded, though he couldn't imagine what they might steal from a farmhouse, other than a meal or two.

"This is what we'll do," Laric said, rubbing his hands together. "You've got an innocent look about you, so you go first. Ask about work as a farmhand. Distract the man of the house. I'll sneak around back and see what they've got inside the place."

"You really think we'll find anything worth taking?"

"Could be a farmwife in there." Laric grinned. Carn rested his hands on his hips.

"Let's try not to hurt anybody."

Laric nodded. "If we don't need to. Take your sword just in case. You might want to hide it in your roll though, so they don't get suspicious."

He clapped Carn on the back and started at a crouch down a ways, along the ridge. He motioned over the rise and Carn started forward. A swathe of summer wheat stretched from right to left some distance and the rhythmic thunk of woodcutting floated to his ears. As he neared the cabin, a few chickens squawked and scattered out of the way. The farmer must have heard them. He came around from the back, axe over one shoulder.

"Not an Ilar?" he said frowning.

Carn frowned back. "Why would I be?"

"On account of there's hardly anyone up in these parts but us and the tribes further north. Unless you're counting Kael and those cutthroats down near Trickle Stream. You aren't one of them, are you?"

Carn blinked. "No, I'm not."

"Then who are you? And what are you doing up here? Deserted from one of the Boundary Forts? An outlaw?" He adjusted that axe. "Don't need that sort of trouble around here. Won't allow it."

"Nothing like that." Carn raised both hands. "I'm just looking for work. Maybe I could lend a hand around the place."

"Lend a hand?"

"I don't need much. Just food and a place to sleep."

"You do look hungry." The farmer seemed to relax. He scratched above one ear. "And there's always work to be done. Truth be told, I wish there were two of you."

No sooner did he say it than a scream sounded from inside the house.

"Marrie!" He started toward the front door, axe in both hands. But Carn moved to block him, hands up in front of him.

"Don't!" he said. "Just run. *Run!*"

"But Marrie?"

"Leave her to me!"

Maybe it was that innocent look Laric had mentioned, but the man actually listened. He turned, bolted off in the direction Carn had just arrived from. Laughter rang from inside the house and as Carn turned, the door burst open and the farmer's wife shot through the front door, almost directly into his arms.

"Ahh!"

Carn caught her, turned her in the direction of her fleeing husband and pushed. "Run!" he hissed.

She watched him over one shoulder for a stride then dashed toward the crest of the ridge where the farmer had turned to wait. A few moments later, Laric came out, a crust of bread in one hand, drawn sword in the other.

"You let her get away?" he said around a mouthful.

"Uh...she's stronger than she looks."

Laric sighed. "Well, I hope Kael will settle for a few chickens."

They took the chickens—those they could catch—a few sets of cutlery, and a fancy comb made of tin. It wasn't much, but Laric said it would have to do.

"He's a miserly sonofabitch, Kael." Laric looked grim. "But he'll like that comb. Yeah, that'll be enough."

Carn frowned, reading the tension in his friend's voice. "Is he that bad? Is that why we need these swords?"

"Still not coming back to you?" Laric sighed, stepped closer to rest a hand on Carn's shoulder. "I guess I gotta prepare you. You see, Kael and his boys, they're some hard men. Outlaws, I heard tell. Murderers a few of them. Kael doesn't turn any man away, or woman, long as they pay in."

Carn felt sick. From more than just the belly-full of stolen lunch.

"Some of 'em aren't so bad." Laric put in hastily. "They're just regular thieves. Like us."

Carn looked around the farmer's little cabin, at the herbs hanging from the rafters, the quilt on the straw-stuffed mattress, the little table with its two chairs. Anywhere but at Laric. A fly buzzed through the open shutters and Carn waved it absently out of his face. "I need to get back to myself. Get my memories."

"We gotta go to Kael," Laric said. "He'll be expecting us."

"I gotta get my memories back first."

"They'll come back. I'm sure they will." But the look on Laric's face betrayed his doubt.

Carn met his eyes. "How far is it to the warlock's cabin?"

Laric didn't talk much this time and they marched in silence. Cresting a final rise of swaying grass, the green expanse of the forest of Ilia appeared before them. In the distance, purple mountains brushed the sky. From what Carn had gathered, the warlock's cabin was only a few miles into the trees.

"We'll have to be quiet once we get in there," Laric said, flicking his head toward the forest. "Shouldn't be any tribesmen about this time of year, but you never know."

Carn nodded. He looked back the way they'd come, remembered the shock on the farmers face, the wide-eyed panic of his wife. Images from the dream—no, *the past*, he realized—flooded his head. Of Hatton, of the raiders, of his parents, gone to Vorda's Halls now.

"Do you ever wish things could be like they were?" he asked.

He didn't have to say more, Laric knew what he meant. "Sometimes."

"You weren't really gonna kill that farmer, were you?"

Laric sniffed. "Well, I'm glad I didn't have to. But better him than us when we get back to Kael."

They started walking again, watching the terrain for any sign of Ilars, swords within easy reach. Their path took them past a few sparse thickets of evergreen and then under the eaves of the forest proper. Something like a dear run led them downhill, across a little creek, back up over a ridge. The trees gave way to a small, eerily quiet meadow, a squat house built of logs and roofed over in turf sitting dead-center.

Carn started toward it, but Laric yanked him back. "He's a warlock, remember? We gotta have a plan."

"I'll go in. You don't have to do this."

Laric muttered a curse. "They don't have back doors, these longhouses. But we can go in together, through the front. A sword against the neck should encourage the bastard to fix your head."

Carn rested a hand on his friend's shoulder. "Just wait outside. I'll call you when it's safe."

Laric's eyes narrowed but he nodded. Carn stepped through the tall grass toward the longhouse, heart racing in his chest, each stride an eternity. When he reached the door, it swung open easily. Ducking his head, he stepped down and inside a low-ceilinged room with a packed earth floor, strewn with animal pelts arranged around a burned-out fire.

"I knew you'd be back, mmmm?"

Carn sucked in a startled breath, looked up to find a spikey-haired Ilar standing in the shadows at the far end of the longhouse. The tribesman stepped from darkness into the light filtering down through the smoke-hole above. Carn's hand went to his hilt at first, but he forced it away, wiped it on the side of his pants.

"Thirsty?" the Ilar asked, extending his hands to offer a skin of water, or maybe wine. Carn was thinking about the odd lilt of the Ilar's accent when memory of that skin hit him, rocked him where he stood. He remembered this place, remembered drinking from it.

Carn licked his lips. "That's it, isn't it? The wine that took my memories." His eyes lifted from the bulging skin to the warlock's eyes. There was sadness there, but patience too.

The spikey-haired tribesman took another step forward, drink extended in his hands.

"I..." Carn stammered.

Laric's voice interrupted from outside. "You alright, Carn?" A pause. "I'm coming in!"

"Wait!" Carn looked up.

The Ilar nodded. "Mmmm," he hummed. He said nothing else, just extended the skin out toward Carn. Carn knew what to do from there.

Reaching forward, he took it in both hands. It was heavy with liquid. He thought of what the farmer had said about helping on the farm, about all the things Laric had told him, about Kael and his lot especially. There really wasn't anything to consider. Turning, he stepped back out through the longhouse door, un-stoppered the skin, and passed it to his friend.

Author's Note

This was a light one as far as action goes. Even so, I think it has value in bringing us back to the reality of what a weapon is capable of, that it can be used for good or evil. In the film AMERICAN SNIPER, the father tells his son, you can be a sheep, a wolf, or the sheepdog. The movie focuses on the metaphorical 'sheepdog' arising from and growing out of wolf-like instincts. In LIVE BY THE SWORD, the focus is on what can make the sheep become wolves.

The forest of Ilia features in each in the first three books in my debut series, the DOG OF WAR Epic. I won't give any spoilers, but let's just say the swords get plenty of use. If you want to read more, join my newsletter by visiting www.deankastle.com and be first to know when it releases. You'll also receive a free bonus story about an assassin known as the Infamous Blacksheep.

Thank you!

-DK

Hard Choices

Palladine stood proud. Heels clicked on worn marble as the queen and her entourage marched toward him, aged columns like sentinels to either side. Marshal Abrem followed behind her, trailed in turn by a pair of guardsmen carrying a huge chest between them. Queen Lyanne drew them to a halt in front of Palladine and the other soldiers at attention.

She smiled at each of them, a slight curve to her perfect pink lips. "Defenders of the ancient and venerable realm of Pellon, today we commend your valor."

She paused long enough for the few scattered noteworthies around the great-hall to offer a brief round of applause.

"Lord Marshal Abrem has personally recommended each of you for the captaincy. So, too, your commander has relayed to me the deeds each of you performed to warrant this honor. I have taken note."

Palladine felt his pulse quicken as the queen's gaze drifted from one end of the line to the other, falling on him last, lingering there. Did he imagine it, or had that smile actually touched her eyes? He tightened his stomach, tried to stand even straighter.

At a wave from Queen Lyanne, the men with the chest came forward. Lord Marshal Abrem moved alongside them, unlatching the chest to draw out a polished bronze cuirass. He stepped up to set this in the hands of the soldier farthest to Palladine's right, murmured some words of encouragement, and announced, "Captain Jouran."

Another brief round of applause and Marshal Abrem moved down the line. The process repeated until he was standing in front of Palladine.

"You could have had this by birthright, Lord Palladine," Abrem said quietly. "Accepted a commission back in the Golden City, leaned on your family name, even as a second son, and kept yourself clear of anything resembling real service. But you came here, to these blight-infested borderlands, and *earned* it."

Palladine met his steady dark gaze with his own cool blue one. The lord marshal offered an approving nod. He turned, took the next cuirass from the chest, and set it in Palladine's hands. "Captain Palladine."

The sound of gentle applause from ahead lifted the new-made captain's eyes. It came from Queen Lyanne herself. Had she really been told of his deeds? It had certainly been a tough, dirty job. But he'd seen it through for the greater good. With the Affliction still plaguing the citizenry, and, of course, the ever-present threat of the Mog, there would be plenty more.

"I have prepared something special for the new captains," Queen Lyanne was saying.

Still standing close to Palladine, the surprise on the lord marshal's face was evident. The queen snapped her fingers at her assistant, a watery-eyed old man, and the pair stepped up to the line of soldiers, captain's cuirass still cradled in the arms of each. She started where Abrem had, looping medals of some sort over each man's head. She arrived in front of Palladine. There was that smile again.

Palladine felt his pulse quicken. She was a striking woman, even if she wasn't young anymore, pale and fine-boned, her perfect dark curls shot through with silver and clasped with gold. The rose-water scent of her filled Palladine's lungs as her arms went over his head, his neck bent so she could reach. She draped her gift across his chest. He'd heard the rumors of witchcraft that surrounded Lyanne, but up close her presence hinted at a very normal, earthly magic, the kind a beautiful woman could summon on a whim.

Or maybe it was just the proximity of such power. True, the Familae Leyai had only recently solidified control of the Lion's Den, but having met her now, Palladine didn't doubt Lyanne had done as much as her husband, King Elius, to fend off Kion and the other families. They were the most powerful rulers in all the Sworn Realms, Lyanne and Elius. As the queen turned, left the hall, Palladine looked down at the medal. A round disc of silver, stamped like a coin, only bigger, with the lion's head of Pellon.

Palladine wasn't much for small talk. He left the other new captains at the barracks to celebrate among themselves and strode out the citadel, new cuirass strapped firmly in place. The pitted stones edifices of Vordae's Old City crowded in close to the fortress walls, among them a row of eateries near the Great Temple frequented exclusively by those of means. Little risk there of the rank and file interrupting a meal.

Eying the gleaming cuirass and medal across Palladine's chest, the doorman at a place called the Hawker's Roost held the entry open. Palladine took a corner table, back to the wall as always, and waved for food and wine. Despite his choice of venue, he was interrupted anyway, but not by a noisy dice game or a brawl, rather by the arrival of Queen Lyanne's watery-eyed assistant.

"Captain Palladine." The aged servant dipped his head. "My mistress, the queen, commends you. She would have you for a private supper. And a few words."

Palladine blinked. Perhaps it wasn't his imagination, he really *had* seen something more in the queen's smile. What she could want from the second son of a declining familae, he could only speculate. Only when the queen's man stood there looking at him did he understand she wanted to see him right now.

He pushed up from his seat. "Of course." The old man turned to lead the way. Palladine ran a hand over the stubble on his mostly bald head, pulled at his cuffs to straighten any wrinkles on his white tabard's sleeves.

He followed the old man back the way he'd come. Passing Vorda's ancient temple—goddess of death and wisdom, and namesake of the city itself—Palladine touched the medal hanging from his neck. Was it wisdom that awaited, or ultimately his death?

He didn't have time to think on it long. Back through the citadel gates, the watery-eyed old man ushered Palladine through tight corridors to a receiving chamber in one of the towers. The queen waited on a padded couch, sandaled feet up to one side.

She swung her legs down and rose when he entered. "Captain Palladine." That smile again. "So pleased you could join me. You look good in that armor. But come, sit here."

She led him to a chair that matched her couch, taking him by the hand, so casual, like it was nothing. Several trays rested on a sideboard and from them she sawed off a few slices of red, juicy beef. Deft fingers picked up a few grapes, a wedge of cheese, set it all on a silver plate and delivered it into his hands.

Palladine's mouth opened and closed. *I've just been served dinner by the Queen of Pellon.*

Lyanne trilled a laugh, like she'd read his mind. "Eat, Captain. Be at ease, we're friends here."

He dipped his head, took a careful bite, made sure to chew with his mouth closed. Back at the sideboard, the queen poured two goblets of wine. She sniffed at one, closed her eyes and smiled, then took a sip.

"From Rath." She walked the second goblet over to Palladine. "A fine vintage."

"Thank you, my queen."

Lyanne settled herself on the couch again, leaning on one arm, slender feet up on the cushions to the other side. "Lord Marshal Abrem told me something of each of the new captains, but your story touched me most. It was a difficult task they set before you, and yet you never wavered."

"It was dangerous, in its own way. Hard choices had to be made, but it wasn't a battle."

"Your reputation as a swordsman is well known, even to me, Captain. I wonder if it would have been easier if it *had* been a fight."

Palladine blinked. "My queen, you flatter me."

"I never flatter."

The way she smiled he knew that was a lie. But it made him smile back.

"Regardless of the action itself," the queen went on, "the assignment, if I may say it, was far beneath the station of a landed man, second son or no."

"Well, with my father's passing, I cannot say that I am landed, my queen. The familae estates reside with my older brother, as is his right."

"Oh? A shame, that." She reached down, arranged the hem of her gown around her ankles. "But let's not mull over such things. We have good food and wine, after all. Please, partake."

Palladine took a few dainty bites. The queen picked at a morsel or two herself, then set her plate aside. She sighed. "It was the hard choices you made that won you the captaincy, you know. That's why you're here. Hard choices, but wise ones."

Palladine nodded. "I've found the easy choice is rarely the right one."

"So true. But do you like your post here in the Lows?"

Palladine wasn't sure how she wanted him to answer. "I do. There are problems here, real ones. And I can fix them, right the wrongs, ensure order and law."

"I'd imagine that can be quite daunting in these oft-times lawless reaches of the realm. No? These days the Lows draw outcasts and fugitives like honey draws flies. Not to mention the barbarian Mog always clawing at our lands. Do you never tire of it, Captain?"

"Do you mean to ask if I miss Paellia, Pellon proper?" Palladine frowned. "Of course. But what's the point of fixing problems any halfwit could fix? Challenges in the Lows mean life or death more times than not. That's where a man proves himself, not in some minister's chamber in the Lion's Den, if you'll forgive me saying it."

She smiled, swung her feet down to step over to the table and fetch more wine. "Exactly. You saved lives in Cahlmet you know, even if it cost lives doing so. Tell me how it all happened."

Palladine met her eyes as she arrived in front of him with the carafe. "Are you sure you want to hear it, my queen? There were children. And I lost good soldiers as well."

"Beyond a doubt. The Affliction is more than just a bad air, you know, like a pox or a wave of grippe. It's a curse."

She let the word hang on the air. Palladine frowned, took a sip of his wine.

"As such," the queen went on, "it is no accident this pestilence finds us. This abomination, you see, was raised by the will of a malevolent circle in the Great South. Sorcerers—magicians you might call them. Or warlocks."

Or witches, Palladine thought.

And how could she know such a thing anyway? Her words were about as close as they could be to admitting she was a witch herself, like the rumors said. He sipped at his wine again to hide his expression.

The queen had turned to settle back onto her couch. "I haven't seen it," she said, "but I'm told it is a horrible ailment, the Affliction. The eyes turn red first, then spots on the skin. There is a fever. A strong man can die of it overnight."

Palladine nodded. "I saw much dying. For a fortnight we quarantined the citizenry in Cahlmet. Some tried to escape. We sent them back...if we could." He didn't say what they did to those who wouldn't turn back, the first few at least, to send a message. He'd watched them die as well.

The queen waved a hand, dismissed it. "Cahlmet was a mixed settlement. Paellians and Mog, half-bloods. Debtors, criminals, and every other sort."

Palladine pursed his lips, looked down into his wine. She spoke truth, and he supposed those children would have grown into nothing better than the dregs from which they were spawned. But he'd lost soldiers too. He took a healthy swallow. *Hard choices indeed.*

Sensing the darkness in his thoughts perhaps, the queen rose, threw open a shutter to let in more light. She stood there soaking it in, spoke to him with her eyes closed, face tilted to receive the sun. She moved easy, casual-like, but this was it, the reason she'd summoned him. Palladine could sense it.

"It's been years since I visited Vordae, did I tell you?" She sighed, turned back to face him. "But I can't say I find it improved. Just yesterday I went to the Great Temple."

Palladine nodded. "A grand and ancient structure, my queen. They say it's even older than the citadel."

"But filled with base creatures." Her eyes fixed on him like an eagle's on its prey, her face half masked in shadow. "I spoke of malevolent circles in the Great South, but there are other circles just as evil and much nearer."

Palladine perked up, sat a little straighter. "Something should be done perhaps."

"I knew you would understand." She moved back to her couch, sitting proper this time, leaning forward as she spoke. "The disciples of the Dark Goddess have grown dark indeed. They forget wisdom and dwell only upon death."

"The brothers and sisters in the Great Temple?"

"Dark circles," the queen said, her voice almost a whisper. "I fear hard choices, as you call them, must be made."

Palladine set his jaw, nodded. He felt compelled to do something. This was the woman that had given him that medal, singled him out, after all. And with this task, his heart told him, as with few others, he'd truly been handed something wrong he could make right.

Not so hard a choice, this one, not for him. "I shall pay them a visit, my queen."

"But tread with caution, Captain. The creatures of the temple are led by a woman, a vile, cunning old hag if ever there was one. And then there is the Elder. He is the weapon in her hand."

"They have guardsmen as well, half dozen at least," Palladine said.

"They are nothing compared to the Elder. And Chaelea. See to them and the power of their circle will be broken."

She rose from her seat, stepped over to the sideboard again. She ignored the food and wine this time but pulled open a drawer to draw something out.

Palladine frowned. It looked like another medal, but hung from a leather cord instead of a ribbon. She moved toward him, lifted it over his head as she had with the last. It sat light against his chest. Looking down, Palladine saw that it was crafted from thin, intertwined slivers of wood, a silver-brown circle with something like a tooth at the center.

"This will protect you," the queen said. "As much as you can be protected."

She arranged the amulet, if it could be called that, in the center of his new cuirass. Taking his hands in hers, she pulled gently until he stood.

She didn't step back, but remained mere inches from him, looking up into his blue eyes with her big dark ones. "I know you will not fail."

Palladine waited until dawn. The power of the Dark Goddess would be waning then, he reasoned, her clerics still bleary-eyed with morning, or at least tired from a night's work. *Doing the gods only knew what.* He moved the queen's amulet so that it hung down his back, hidden under his cloak, and left his quarters at the barracks.

The Great Temple was a squat stone structure, heavy-walled and fortress-like except for the absence of any towers. Its charcoal-colored granite stones stood out among the sandy yellow limestone used everywhere else, each block as tall as a man, as if their ancestors, the Old Aturians, had employed giants to build it. From the front, it stood bluff and inscrutable, but along the sides, narrow windows stretched from ground level several floors up, ending in peaked arches. The front gates—three of them—opened under peaked arches as well. The cast-bronze doors of the middle one stood open.

A black-garbed guardsman inside the doorway barely glanced at Palladine as he stepped through into a high-ceilinged antechamber. Nothing out of the ordinary for a man in armor and with a sword to visit, not in the Lows. A channel set in the floor flowed with dark water, the wan light of daybreak rippling pink on the surface. Palladine crossed over on the creaky iron gangway, a symbol of crossing into the lands of the dead.

He glanced left, then right. Corridors led to the libraries in one direction, the private living quarters of the temple's denizens in the other, the queen had told him. Straight ahead, a tall doorway with the same peaked arch above led to the inner sanctum. He pushed through into a huge dark chamber.

The door boomed shut behind him, its echo betraying the enormous size of the chamber even if Palladine's eyes couldn't see anything. An opening in the roof, high above, let in a meager, diffuse glow, filtering down to the center of the room. As Palladine's eyes adjusted, he made out the shape of a man standing over a dark slab directly beneath it.

Left hand casual on his hilt, he strode forward. He *felt* more than saw, shapes standing to either side, shuffling this way and that. As he neared the center of the sanctum, he was able to make out the pale bald head of an old cleric. *The Elder.*

Palladine's heart quickened. There was only one thing that could be done, a difficult thing, but necessary. A hard choice. He felt the talisman between his shoulder blades as he walked. His left hand pulled ever so slightly on his sword to loosen it in the sheath.

"Elder?" he asked, arriving to face him across what appeared to be a rough-cut block of basalt.

"You are troubled, my child." The old man frowned, shaved eyebrows pinched. "A mist surrounds you. Why do you hide?"

"I bear a message," Palladine said. "From the queen."

In one arcing motion, his sword was out, flashing over the basalt slab and splashing it with gore as the blade hacked halfway through the old man's neck. Impossibly, he staggered but didn't go down. His eyes locked with Palladine's and he snarled, raising a long, evil-looking knife, but the captain swung again, separating head from shoulders.

The queen's amulet burned against Palladine's back and he hissed, clawed at it with his left hand. The motion turned him in time to meet an onrushing guard, garbed in black like the others and nearly invisible in the half-light.

"You!"

Palladine didn't need to see more than a shadow to anticipate the slash coming toward him. He met it with a two-handed parry, followed by a swift lunge, impaling the guard. His sword pulled free and he stepped clear as the man collapsed forward, hit the floor with a thud.

"Chaelea," he muttered to himself, turning a circle in the gloom. A second guardsman appeared before he could decide which way to go, and steel rang against steel as Palladine surged forward to meet him.

"Heretic!" the man spat. The guardsman swung again, sword flashing bright, but easily deflected. Palladine circled, steered the man back toward the basalt altar with cut and thrust. When the dark form of the first, fallen guard appeared behind the second, Palladine pressed, drove him into a backpedal until he tripped over the corpse with a curse.

A skip forward and a downward thrust silenced him. Palladine heard the shouts of other guards, but he dashed toward the back of the hall, hoping to find the woman, Chaelea, there. An inconspicuous door led into what appeared to be living quarters, where several more clerics with the shaved eyebrows of the devout scrambled this way and that.

Hard choices. He cut them down, whoever he could catch, black robes stabbed through the back, cut across the front as he sent them to their goddess. Perhaps he did them a favor. Perhaps it wasn't a hard choice at all. Either way, it was the will of the queen, and therefore the law.

"Be still, warrior's heart!" a woman's voice boomed. Palladine felt the queen's amulet burn into his back. He writhed, clawed at it with his left hand, turning at the same time to find a tall, wraith-like outline standing in the doorway he'd entered through. The heat of the amulet began to fade and Palladine felt his legs going weak, but she was too far away to reach. In desperation, he hurled his sword, axe-like, end over end.

It didn't maim or kill her, but it didn't miss either. "Ahh!" She stumbled. It was enough.

Palladine felt his heart skip a beat, then start pounding again like it might burst out of his chest. He charged across the room, leaping over the body of a dead cleric to tackle Chaelea to the ground. His forehead hit something hard as they landed, stunned him, and then they were all tearing limbs, scratching, punching clawing, the both of them.

A hand closed on Palladine's throat, the bony grip far too strong to belong to any woman. He rolled so that he was on top, but the fingers on his neck didn't loosen a hair. He pummeled at the woman's skull, a hideous, hairless thing smeared with blood. Eyes like grey storm clouds pierced him and her lips cracked in a red smile. His vision went bright, started to fade, but one hand found his belt knife in time, plunged it into her side, again and again until the grip on his neck relented.

He rolled to one side, coughed, struggled for air. He heard the creature, Chaelea, rising behind him. Scrabbling to his feet, Palladine turned to face her. The hilt of his knife stood out from the side of her black robes, but she came forward, inexorable as Death itself, her mistress. Chaelea's mouth turned up in a smile, and she laughed, a thin, reedy noise. As he watched, she pulled his knife out of her side and turned the point toward him.

"That bitch would bare her claws against me?" Chaelea hissed. "*Me*?"

Palladine eyes searched wildly for a weapon, landed on a candelabra resting on a sideboard. He lunged toward it, but Chaelea flicked out a hand toward one of the dead men on the floor. An arm came up to claw at Palladine. He whimpered like a child, recoiled, back against the wall.

This was an evil like nothing he'd ever seen. Worse than the blood-thirsty Mog, worse than the Affliction, worse than the men that had come and collected from his father until the man had wept and hid in the cellar. An abomination, a stain to be cleansed, a wrong that must be made right. Palladine touched his captain's cuirass, steeled himself as Chaelea came closer. When the distance was right, he dove at that knife, chest first.

"Eiii!" The sorceress—she could be nothing else—shrieked a wordless curse as the weapon crunched against him, the pair of them flying sideways. The blade squealed, scraping along bronze, but the armor held. The knfe slid off the edge finally, slicing the front of Palladine's arm as they crashed to the ground once more.

This time, Palladine found Chaelea's hands before they could find him. He pinned them to the ground. She thrashed like a wild thing, red spittle flying from her white lips. He brought up a knee, planted it down on her knife-hand and she snapped at his groin with her teeth, her sinuous neck almost long enough to reach. But with his free left hand, Palladine punched her square in the face, once, twice, a third time until she was dazed. He reached down, stripped her fingers back to steal the knife, and plunged it straight through an eye.

The morning sun shined dazzlingly bright as Palladine staggered back out into the street, returned from the realm of the dead to the land of the living. The remaining guardsmen, if there were any, had fled. Passersby going about their morning business steered wide around him, gawked, hurried back the way they had come. Palladine blinked, realized he was holding a bloody sword. He sheathed it and started toward the citadel.

Shocked sentries at the gate rushed down to check on him but Palladine waved them off. "Tell the queen I have returned." He moved in a daze in the direction of the same audience chamber where she'd received him the day before. Her watery-eyed manservant admitted him, then closed the door and left him there.

Queen Lyanne arrived through an entrance in the rear, hands on her cheeks. "Oh, Captain, are you hurt?" She hurried forward to settle him on her couch. He knew he hadn't escaped the Great Temple unscathed but looked down to see blood running down his wrist—*a lot* of blood—dripping off his fingers from the cut on his arm. He felt a pain in the center of his back where her amulet had burned him as well. His new captain's cuirass was stained red.

"I'm alright."

She moved behind him to remove his cloak, draw the amulet and cord over his head, and unbuckle his armor. She let them drop to the floor. The cuirass she rested on top of the cloak, the amulet on top of that, nothing but a burnt husk hanging from a string, like something pulled from a campfire.

"It is done," he said.

The queen came back around to the front of the couch. She took his face in her hands. "I know." She leaned forward and before he knew what was happening, her lips were against his, her tongue in his mouth.

He tried to pull away. "I—" he stammered.

But the queen pushed him down on his back. Deft hands worked his belt, pulled on his tabard. She was a beautiful woman, even in her middle years, and Palladine's body reacted accordingly. Her skirts went up and she threw a leg over to straddle him. As she kissed him, he remembered the old wives' tale of a witch using her body to enslave a man. But she was already on top of him, grinding. They wanted the same thing anyway, the queen and him; to do what was right.

Queen Lyanne did not call him back to her audience chamber the next day, or the day after that. On the third day, her retinue left for the Golden City. Except for the polished cuirass he wore, for Palladine, it all could have been a dream.

Instead of leading patrols into the Mog waste, however, now he assigned them. He assembled with the other captains, marshals, and ministers in the citadel's war room when they met. He ate and drank among them as well, proven warriors of good bloodlines, like him.

Two weeks later, word reached him that his brother had died, leaving him owner of the familae estate, humble as it was. A few days after that, a letter sealed with the cat of Familae Leyai, together with the lion of the Sworn Realm of Pellon, arrived. Palladine took this to his chambers in the officers' barracks to open in private. He wasn't familiar with the handwriting, but he could hear Lyanne's voice in his head as he read.

Esteemed Captain Palladine,

I hope this letter finds you well, even in this joyless time. It has been reported to me that your brother has died, for which I offer my deepest sympathy.

You have accomplished much in Vordae, and throughout the Lows, but with this tragedy, I'm sure you'll want to return to Pellon proper to attend to family affairs. I have arranged for you to remain in Paellia after, if you so wish. A captaincy in the first host, attached to the palace, has been prepared. It would please me to have a dependable soldier of your caliber close at hand. There is much good that can be done here in the Golden City by someone who does not shy away from the hard choices.

Again, I express my sympathies. I know you will consider the post in Paellia as well.

L

Those words tumbled through his head, and he sank onto the edge of his bunk. He hadn't told anyone, but on the inside, he was unsettled by Matheu's death. No matter that they'd never really gotten along, that he'd always viewed the man as a younger version of their father, a frivolous spender likely to finish the job and bankrupt the familae altogether.

As for the queen, she wanted him to accept the post in Paellia, that much was clear. And a position with the first host, stationed in Paellia's citadel, was nothing to scoff at.

Palladine was no fool though; a half-wit would wonder at the timing of Matheu's death. And yet the man was already dead, what was the point of wasting more thought on it?

And even if the queen was somehow involved, was it not for the greater good, bringing him to the Golden City to aid her, and to save the familae fortune at the same time?

Palladine stood up, stepped to the washbasin on its stand and looked down into his reflection. He'd done some wrong, some evil, there could be no question about that. He'd slept with a married woman, killed men and women both, and let others die. Some of them innocents, some of them children.

Others weren't innocent at all though. A shiver ran down his spine thinking of the Elder and of the sorceress, Chaelea. Surely their deaths were well-warranted. As for the others, the guardsmen, the clerics, the folk of Cahlmet, it was all for a greater good, wasn't it?

In the washbasin, Palladine's reflection looked back at him, stern blue eyes, stubbly head and jaw. Beneath his face, the polished bronze of his cuirass peeked just over the rim of the bowl.

No, the gods had rewarded him, he decided, raised him up. Surely that meant he'd done what was just. From beside the washbasin, he lifted a razor, scraped his cheeks first and his scalp, until all was smooth and clean. Shavings fell into the water, distorted his reflection, but soon he was done. He'd need to look his best after all, when he arrived in the Golden City.

Author's Note

Swords and sorcery just go together, like beer and pizza, don't they? With this one, the idea was to explore how a lawman's principles might lead him astray. And, of course, to write in some good old-fashioned fisticuffs while I was at it.

Captain Palladine gets plenty of 'screen-time' in my debut series, the DOG OF WAR Epic. His origins were always in my thoughts. As I wrote DOG OF WAR, the story of his first interaction with Queen

Lyanne tickled the back of my mind. I had to put it into words. I hope the telling entertained you.

If you've been reading the notes after each story, you already know you can join my newsletter at www.deankastle.com to receive another story for free, additional bonus content, and updates regarding the release of my novels DOG OF WAR, HAIR OF THE DOG, and DOG DAYS. Assuming you liked what you read, there's plenty more where that came from in these, the first three books of the series. Keep reading for an excerpt from book one and a small taste of what the series holds.

I sincerely hope you enjoyed reading these stories as much as I enjoyed writing them.

All the best,

DK

An Excerpt from DOG OF WAR

A low-burning campfire lit the circle of faces red, chased shadows across dirty white tabards and pitted iron blades. Geth sat shoulder to shoulder among the other so-called soldiers, but as the new man kept quiet, listening with hidden contempt to the tales being told.

"It's one thing to kill a man in a dust-up," their pock-faced sergeant was saying. "It's something else to look him in the eye and cut his throat. Traitors, wounded men, prisoners—" he flicked a significant glance at the greasy-haired captive in their charge. "The gods know I've bled my share."

The men to Geth's left and right hooted. It only took one glance at their shifty eyes and sunken knuckles to peg that lot. Conmen. Outlaws. Cut-throat murderers. The kind that would sell their own sister for a copper, their mother for two.

But in the wake of the Affliction, with more dead to be buried than living to swing the shovels, rats like these had all left their hiding-holes. Geth stole a glance at the prisoner they'd been scraped together to guard over, shackled beside the row of tethered horses. Now *there* was a true rogue. Blue eyes met his dark ones and the big warrior spit a curse.

"What are you looking at?" Quick as a whip, he hurled the rabbit thigh he'd been gnawing at to pelt the prisoner across the cheek. The little thief scrambled to retrieve it, devouring the morsel like an animal.

That brought the gaze of the sergeant swinging toward Geth. "How 'bout you, half-breed? Bet you've settled a score or two with a stab in someone's back."

Derisive laughter echoed around the fire. Geth did his best to look cowed.

For some reason, the sergeant hated him. Even more than he hated everyone else. Perhaps it was the patterns of swirling ink on each forearm, peeking out of Geth's cuffs, marking him at least part Mog and a foreigner. Perhaps, noting his height and broad shoulders, the sergeant feared him as a rival. Or perhaps the old bastard was just filled with more ire than blood and piss combined.

Whatever the reason, Geth ignored the jeers. He reached for the stewpot on its tripod for another pull off the carcass. Someone chucked a gnawed-on bone that struck him full in the face and tumbled down the front of his white tabard.

"That's right, hide under your collar!" someone sneered as he ducked, too late.

"Big dumb bastard!"

Geth blew out a long breath, reined in his temper.

"Well, if it's tales you want, I suppose I've killed a scratch or two."

"I'll bet he has," Pock-face cut in. "A woman once, while she was sleeping."

More laughter.

But Geth raised his voice over it. "I've never been in the army as we are now," he lied, "but I've bloodied a blade more than once over the years. Been to the east, where the wild men breathe fire and tattoo their skin with devilish patterns. And I did a stretch in Turia, where they make the finest blades and remember an insult for decades and more. I've sailed with an Iyrund slave-trader from Halicarn clear across Longsea, and yet I've sent just as many souls to Vorda's keeping in the alleyways and dark corners of our own Golden City."

"Golden *bloody* City," someone echoed and spat.

"Better for a tavern-tale than a tavern brawl I'd wager," Pock-face snorted.

But every eye had fixed on Geth. They wanted tales and he had plenty. He found himself warming to the task.

He spoke of blood-soaked battlefields and feuds ended with stealthy midnight murder. Of crushing a slave rebellion and being forced to wear the chains himself. Eyes widened around the fire at the most gruesome descriptions of war's true horrors and the matter-of-fact delivery of the butcher who gave the telling. Those were the first truths to be spoken that night, Geth was sure of it. He'd just started in on his days as a pit-fighter in Adamar when a voice from behind cut him off.

"That's enough."

The shaved white pate of Palladine, their captain, materialized out of the darkness beside the horses. Firelight gleamed red on a cuirass polished to perfection as the unblinking stare of a real soldier swept over them. Their greasy-haired prisoner shied away. Geth cursed himself for being so absorbed in his own voice he hadn't heard the captain arrive.

Pock-face sprang up to salute him, a gesture copied hastily by everyone else. "Just having a bit of a laugh, my lord." The sergeant jabbed a thumb in Geth's direction. "This big whoreson was telling us how many women he's killed."

Palladine's gaze fell on Geth, taking in every detail. Geth tugged down at his cuffs lest his tattoos make notice.

"I suggest you all take your rest," Palladine said. "We wake before dawn. It's twenty miles to Sorn. The Tower of the Moon awaits."

At mention of the Tower, their greasy-haired captive moaned. Reserved for only the worst offenders, that prison was kept pitch black during the day. Each night, however, the moonlight was let in through a hole in the roof. They said it could drive a man mad.

Palladine didn't mentioned it by accident either, he knew what sort of men he led. He wanted them to know he had the power to see that their road ended in the Tower as well.

Pock-face rounded on Geth. "You heard the captain, enough of your lies. You take first watch. To bed with the rest of you. Don't make me say it twice!"

"Yessir."

But Geth hid a smile as Palladine turned and the clop of horse's hooves faded into the distance. The captain had decided to ride on to the next town in search of lodgings befitting someone of his rank. And away from the carnage that was about to unfold.

How many tyrants had Geth called master over the thirty some years of his life? How many men had used him, mistreated him, haughty as Captain Palladine or hateful as old Pock-face? *Too many*. Geth slid the tripod and remains of their rabbit stew back over the fire, stoked the flames. He made no attempt to suppress such memories. He welcomed them.

"Bastards," he muttered. "Back-stabbing cowards. Lying thieves..."

He listened for the rhythmic breathing of Pock-face and the other four guards. The pot had begun to tremble, threatened to boil over. Rising with care not to make a sound, he drew his sword quietly from its sheath then took the end of his cloak in the other hand to lift the steaming pot from its hook and spill it full in the sergeant's face.

"*Ahhhhhh!*"

The agony of that scream startled the other four from their sleep. Geth turned from the writhing sergeant to run through the nearest of his bleary-eyed companions. His blade darted in and out, swept to one side to stab the back of a second as he rolled from his bedroll, struggled to rise. The third raised his hands in plea for mercy but Geth chopped through upraised forearm and skull alike. The last of his pathetic, would-be companions tried to run, got tangled in his blankets and was hacked down from behind. That left only Pock-face.

"Mongrel bastard!" he cursed. Even with half his head a burned, swollen mess, the sergeant had managed to gain his feet and draw his sword. Geth turned to face him across the fire.

But old Pock-face hadn't lived to sprout those gray hairs without a few tricks of his own. One foot kicked the flames, the burst of glowing embers blinding Geth so he barely caught the arc of the sergeant's left arm as he hurled a knife. Geth twisted, felt the blade brush past his shoulder.

He wasted no time with words. With a lightness of foot that always took his enemies by surprise, Geth circled toward Pock-face's maimed eye. A nimble pass of his sword from right hand to left allowed him to thrust past a desperate, blind parry, piercing tabard, mail, and flesh.

The sergeant grunted, tried to return a backhanded swing, but Geth caught his wrist with his free hand. He pulled him in close, rammed his sword blade deeper, twisted. That grunt turned to a squeal. Pock-face's one good eye met Geth's and his lips worked, tried but failed to utter one last curse.

Geth spit in his face. With a yank, his sword came free. Pock-face collapsed in a heap like a puppet with cut strings. Blood dripped from

Geth's hand, and he wiped it on his white, army-issue tabard as he moved toward the wagon where the greasy-haired prisoner waited.

"You're not going to kill me too, are you?"

Geth smiled. Tossing his sword down, he stooped to pick up an axe that had belonged to one of the others. He could only imagine how he looked, blood splattered, still panting, axe in hand. The prisoner knelt, stretched his shackled hands out in front of his face. The thrown rabbit thigh had left a red welt on his cheek, but he smiled right back as Geth worked the axe-head, hacked through the chains that bound him.

These scenes represent a sample of my debut novel, DOG OF WAR. To continue reading Geth's adventure, visit www.deankastle.com and download the series. I hope you enjoyed this excerpt and all the rest!

-DK

ABOUT THE AUTHOR

Dean Kastle is the author of SWORD SONGS, the DOG OF WAR Epic, and other works. In addition to his love of 'story' in every medium, he's a rabid foodie and soccer fanatic. As far as Dean's concerned, Pluto is still a planet, and the oxford comma is a matter of taste. He doesn't wear a beret or write with a fountain pen, but he does own a life-size replica of the Iron Throne. From that perch, he plots the next tale of warfare, adventure, and betrayal. Readers can connect with Dean at www.deankastle.com, by joining his newsletter, on X, or on Facebook. He lives in fly-over country with his wife, three kids and (yes) a dog.

www.ingramcontent.com/pod-product-compliance
Lightning Source LLC
Chambersburg PA
CBHW022048170626
46808CB00003B/1400